Peppa Goes to Ireland

Peppa and George were packing their suitcases ready to go to Ireland for an Irish-dancing festival. Peppa was so excited she couldn't stop dancing!

This book belongs to

....

LADYBIRD BOOKS

UK | USA | Canada | Ireland | Australia | India | New Zealand | South Africa

Ladybird Books is part of the Penguin Random House group of companies
whose addresses can be found at global.penguinrandomhouse.com.

www.penguin.co.uk   www.puffin.co.uk   www.ladybird.co.uk

Penguin
Random House
UK

First published 2021
001

Licensed by

Printed in China

The authorized representative in the EEA is Penguin Random House Ireland,
Morrison Chambers, 32 Nassau Street, Dublin D02 YH68

A CIP catalogue record for this book is available from the British Library

ISBN: 978-0-241-48715-0

All correspondence to:
Ladybird Books, Penguin Random House Children's
One Embassy Gardens, 8 Viaduct Gardens, London SW11 7BW

MIX
Paper from
responsible sources
FSC
www.fsc.org
FSC® C018179

"How will we get to Ireland, Daddy?" she asked.
"Will we dance all the way there?"
Daddy Pig laughed. "No, Peppa. Ireland is a long
way away. We need to fly or take a boat."

"Hmm," said Mummy Pig. "I don't think we'll fit everything on an aeroplane."
"Do we really need all this?" asked Daddy Pig.
Mummy Pig nodded. "You never know what will come in handy on holiday!"

"OK," said Daddy Pig. "We'll take the ferry instead."
"We can't take a fairy, Daddy!" gasped Peppa. "A fairy
is too small to carry us!"
"Not a *fairy*, Peppa," said Daddy Pig. "A *ferry*. It's a
big boat that can carry cars and people."
"Oh!" said Peppa. "That's much better!"

Once Mummy and Daddy Pig had squeezed everything into the car, they set off for the ferry port.
"*We're going to Ireland!*" sang Peppa excitedly while practising her Irish-dancing steps. "Madame Gazelle said I must rehearse my dancing."

"There's not really room in the car for dance practice, Peppa," said Daddy Pig. "We're a bit squished!"

When they reached the port, Daddy Pig
drove their little car inside the enormous
ferry that was waiting to take them to Ireland.
"It's a bit bigger than Grandpa's boat!" said Peppa.

BUUUUURRRRRRRR!
The ferry honked loudly.
"Just a bit!" Daddy Pig shouted over the noise.

On the ferry crossing, Peppa and George went out on to the deck.
Peppa spotted Ireland in the distance.
"It's so lovely and **green!**" she cried.
"Isn't it beautiful?" said Daddy Pig.
"People call Ireland the Emerald Isle because it's green like an emerald."

"Mummy looks a bit green, too," said Peppa. "Are you feeling all right, Mummy?"

"The sea's a bit choppy for me today," said Mummy Pig.

When they reached
Ireland, the sat nav gave
Daddy Pig directions to
the Irish-dancing festival.
"Follow the winding roads
in and out, in and out . . .
then up and down and over
the hills," it said.

After a while, Daddy Pig stopped the car so
they could have a proper look around.
Peppa and George practised their Irish dancing,
up and down and over the hills.

As they got to the top of the biggest hill, Peppa spotted
Miss Rabbit in a souvenir shop.
"Hello, Miss Rabbit!" said Peppa. "What are you doing here?"
"Hello, Peppa," said Miss Rabbit. "I'm selling souvenirs."

"Look at the Irish-dancing outfits!" gasped Peppa. "Can we get some for the Irish-dancing festival, Daddy? *Pleeeeeaassse!*"
"OK," Daddy Pig said. "Four Irish-dancing outfits, please. They can be our little bit of green Ireland to take home!"

Mummy Pig looked at the other things Miss Rabbit was selling. "Oooh," she said, "I've always wanted one of those, and one of those, and . . ."

Soon, Mummy Pig had bought one of everything in Miss Rabbit's souvenir shop. "Are you sure we have room for all this in the car?" asked Daddy Pig.
"Don't worry," said Mummy Pig, "I'll find a way to fit it all in."

After Mummy Pig's expert packing, Daddy Pig
continued the journey along the winding roads.
"Are we at the festival yet?" asked Peppa.
"I think it's just around this bend," said Daddy Pig.
Peppa looked eagerly out of the window. "It's not!
Are we at the festival yet, now?"
"I think it's just around *this* bend," said Daddy Pig.

Peppa looked out of the window
again. "No," she sighed. "It's not."

"Will it be much longer?" asked Peppa.
"Why don't we ask the sat nav?"
suggested Mummy Pig.
"Your destination is around the
next bend," said the sat nav.

Ha!
Ha!
Ha!

When they finally arrived at the Irish-dancing festival,
the sat nav said, "You have reached your destination."
"Hooray!" everyone cheered.
"It's a bit quiet," said Peppa as they got out
of the car. "Why can't we hear any music?"

At the festival stage, they found Miss Rabbit again.
"I'm afraid we might have to cancel the festival," she said.
"Some of the band have forgotten their instruments."

"Oh no!" Peppa said. But then she had a thought ..."What instruments do they need?"
"An accordion, a tin whistle and a fiddle," said Miss Rabbit.
"I think we might have those in our car!" cried Peppa.

Mummy and Daddy Pig checked the car and pulled out . . .
an accordion, a tin whistle and a fiddle!
"You never know what will come in handy on holiday!"
said Mummy Pig, smiling.
"That's very true, Mummy Pig," said Daddy Pig.

Miss Rabbit gathered everyone at the festival together. "Thanks to Peppa and her family, the Irish-dancing festival can now begin!" she said. "Hooray!" everyone cheered.

Peppa and her family changed into their Irish-dancing outfits.
The band played their music and everyone started dancing.
"Irish dancing is the best!" cried Peppa. "I just can't stop!"
"Me neither!" said Daddy Pig, going quite red.

"You're not green like Ireland, Daddy," said Peppa. "You're red!"
Daddy Pig chuckled. "Thanks, Peppa."

Everyone was having so much fun dancing, they didn't notice it was beginning to rain. Luckily, Miss Rabbit appeared with a basket full of welly boots.

"It's getting a bit too muddy to dance now," said Miss Rabbit, frowning.
"Yes," said Peppa. "But it's the perfect amount of muddy to do this . . ."

...Splat!
"What a wonderful idea!" said Miss Rabbit.
Everyone at the Irish-dancing festival jumped
up and down in muddy puddles with Peppa!

Hee!

Hee!

Hee!

Splat!

Peppa and her family love Ireland ...
and they love jumping up and down
in Irish muddy puddles!

More great Peppa Pig picture books to collect!

 Peppa's Countdown to Bedtime

 Peppa Loves Easter

 Peppa's Best Birthday Party

 George's Tractor

 Peppa's Night Before Christmas

 Peppa Loves Doctors and Nurses

 Peppa is Super!

 Peppa's Summer Holiday

 Peppa's Spooky Halloween

 Peppa Loves Our Planet

 Peppa's Fairy Tale

 Peppa in Space

 Peppa the Mermaid

 I Love You, Daddy Pig!

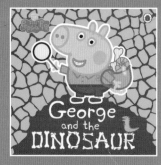 George and the Dinosaur

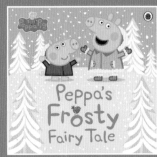 Peppa's Frosty Fairy Tale

 Peppa's Magical Unicorn

 I Love You, Mummy Pig!

 Peppa Meets Father Christmas

 Peppa Goes to London

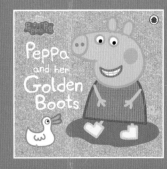 Peppa and her Golden Boots

 Goodnight Peppa

 Let's go Shopping Peppa

 Happy Birthday Peppa!

 The Biggest Muddy Puddle in the World

Peppa and George are going to Ireland for an Irish-dancing festival! But when the band forget their instruments, will Peppa and her family be able to save the day?

U.K. £6.99
ISBN 978-0-241-48715-0
9 780241 487150
90000
www.penguin.co.uk
ebook available